THE ELEPHANT'S WRESTLING MATCH

THE ELEPHANT'S WRESTLING MATCH

by Judy Sierra

illustrated by Brian Pinkney

DUTTON Lodestar Books NEW YORK

Library of Congress Cataloging-in-Publication Data

Sierra, Judy.

The elephant's wrestling match/by Judy Sierra: illustrated by
Brian Pinkney

p. cm.
Summary: Of all the animals challenged by the mighty elephant, only a
tiny bat is able to defeat him in a battle of wits.
ISBN 0-525-67366-0
[1. Animals—Fiction. 2. Pride and vanity—Fiction.]
I. Pinkney, J. Brian, ill. II. Title.
PZ7.S5773E1 1992

[E]—dc20
91-8107 CIP AC

Published in the United States by Lodestar Books,
an affiliate of Dutton Children's Books,
a division of Penguin Books USA Inc.
375 Hudson Street, New York, New York 10014,

Published simultaneously in Canada by
McClelland & Stewart, Toronto

Editor: Virginia Buckley   Designer: Marilyn Granald, LMD

Printed in Hong Kong
First Edition   10 9 8 7 6 5 4 3 2 1

for Christopher R, connoisseur of stories
J.S.

to my friend Seth
B.P.

The mighty elephant stamped his feet,
One, two, three, four.
"No one," he roared, "can bring *me* down!
I challenge all the animals,
Great and small,
To a wrestling match."

The monkey sent the message with his talking drum. "What animal is brave enough, What animal is strong enough, To wrestle with the mighty elephant?"

The she-leopard came to try.
Wrapped her tail around a tree trunk,
And reared up on her hind legs.
She bared her long, sharp claws.

The elephant lifted a leg
And tapped her gently.
The she-leopard fell to the ground.
"Elephant, mighty elephant,
Put the long-clawed leopard in the dust,"
The monkey beat on his drum.
"What animal is brave enough,
What animal is strong enough,
To wrestle with the mighty elephant?"

The crocodile crawled out of the river
Counting his teeth.
He opened his mouth wide and hissed.

The elephant took a step,
Rolled the crocodile over,
And stroked the crocodile's belly with his trunk.
The crocodile smiled and fell asleep.

"Elephant, mighty elephant,
Tamed the fierce crocodile,
Put the long-clawed leopard in the dust,"
The monkey beat on his drum.
"What animal is brave enough,
What animal is strong enough,
To wrestle with the mighty elephant?"
The rhinoceros charged forward.
With his great huge horn
He would bring the elephant crashing down.

He circled around
And hit the elephant from the side.
The elephant swayed
　　and staggered
　　　　and fell . . .
On top of the rhinoceros.

"Elephant, mighty elephant,
Oh, he crushed the rhinoceros,
Tamed the fierce crocodile,
Put the long-clawed leopard in the dust,"
The monkey's drum rang out.
"What animal is brave enough,
What animal is strong enough,
To wrestle with the mighty elephant?"

Down flew a tiny bat.

"I challenge you, mighty elephant."

"You are too small," said the elephant.

"I am not."

"You are too weak," said the elephant.

"I am not."

"I will not wrestle with you," said the elephant.

"Are you afraid?"

"No!" shouted the elephant.

"Let us wrestle."

The elephant swung his trunk at the bat,
But the bat was too quick for him.
She flew
        inside
              the elephant's ear.
The elephant heard a rattle and a buzz.
Suddenly
There was a great pain in his ear.
He shook his head back and forth.
But it did no good.
The tiny bat flapped inside
The great elephant's ear.

At last, the elephant dropped to the ground,
And rubbed his poor, sore ear in the dirt.
The bat flew away to her cave,
Calling the call of victory.
"The bat has done it!
Yes, The bat has done it.
Tiny bat has wrestled
The mighty elephant to the ground,"
The monkey beat on his drum.

The elephant arose, angry.
He grabbed the monkey's drum
And smashed it.
That is why, nowadays,
You don't see monkeys playing the talking drum.
If you want to give the elephant a good scare,
Just tell him that the bat, the tiny bat,
Is coming to wrestle him.

Note on the Talking Drum

The talking drum in this story has an hourglass shape, with drumheads on each end. These are connected with laces that the drummer squeezes to produce different tones as the drum is beaten with a curved stick. The drummer uses the talking drum to imitate the rhythm and tone of speech, and listeners learn to guess what the drum is "saying." Talking drums were once used to send messages over long distances, to convey insults during wrestling matches, and to announce the winners of these matches to neighboring villages.

This story is retold from a folktale of the Bulu people, Cameroon, Africa, which was published in the *Journal of American Folklore*, volume 27 (1914).

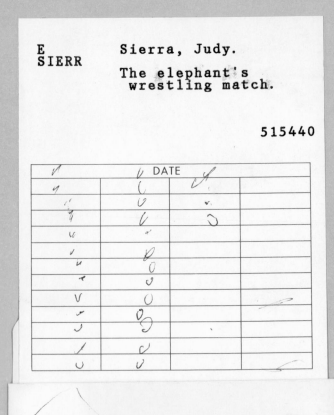